Dragoman Bloodgrue

Volume V: Rulings

By *Rusty Knight*

With *Inevitable Unicorn Press*

Dragoman Bloodgrue
Volume V, Rulings

Welcome to our serial stories!

If you're not familiar with our serials, think of them as a favorite nighttime program that continues with new episodes, only this is in a print format. These are stories that don't necessarily have an end planned for them, or if they do, it's a long way off unlike many television series that we get interested in, only to have them go off air.

Serial stories are a great way to keep you entertained and on edge waiting to see what will happen next, in short enough episodes to enjoy on a lunch break, or before going to bed. Although our stories are designed to be read one episode at a time, unlike TV stories, if you just can't wait for the next episode, you can get another one any time.

Be sure to download episodes when you purchase them!

It is a good idea to download the episode when you first purchase them. Then, you can read them at your leisure.

Please feel free to let us know what you think of our serial stories. It's a trend that may take some getting used to, but we've had positive feedback with them.

Now, it's time to enjoy!
From *InUPress*,

We would like to acknowledge the following for their work in the production of this series.

The author is, *Rusty Knight*
Our cover design is by, *Rusty Knight*
The editing is by, Donna Shumaker (Aria)
Publishing and distribution is by, *InUPress.ca*

Dragoman Bloodgrue
Volume V, Rulings

Dragoman Bloodgrue
Volume V, Rulings

Contents

Rusty Knight

Rusty Knight is a writer who also builds and repairs computers when he is not building blogs and web pages. *Rusty Knight's* writings tend towards the fantasy or sci-fi genres, but he has won an award as best new poet of the year from the American Poetry Society in the early 1980's. *Rusty Knight* is the lead moderator and administrator for the local writing group, Fellowship of the Scribblers.

Currently, *Rusty Knight* is working on a fantasy novel titled, *Laret*, due out in 2017. Rusty grew up on a mixed farm and he has the heart and soul of a self-sufficient farmer, thus he finds he is able to step into all the roles of most characters in his world. Coming from a family of ten in a small five room house, he knows the world of no privacy, so he can relate to the world of Quantos well.

Follow *Rusty Knight* at www.inupress.ca
Please feel free to leave a review at: www.inupress.ca

Dragoman Bloodgrue
Volume V, Rulings

As producer at *InUPress.ca* and author of the *Dragoman Bloodgrue* serial short-story series, I present to you for reading *Dragoman Bloodgrue Volume 5: Rulings* by *Rusty Knight*.

The *Dragoman Bloodgrue Volume* series will be continued in February 2017 with *Dragoman Bloodgrue Volume 6: Servile*

Dalan e-zine Volume 1, Issues one through four can also can be found on *InUPress.ca* with other works, that can also be found at such places as: **Amazon, Kobo, Goodreads, Niume and Scriggler.**

E-books, Kindle and paperback books in the *Dragoman Bloodgrue* series are available at *www.inupress.ca*, **Kindle, Kobo and also on Amazon:**

Bloodgrue Volume 1: Fare Where!
Bloodgrue Volume 2: Breaths
Bloodgrue Volume 3: Business
Bloodgrue Volume 4: Attractions
Dragoman Bloodgrue Volume 5: Rulings

As producer at *InUPress.ca* and author of the *Dragoman Bloodgrue*, **Markus** and the **Lanis,** free serial short-story series, I thank you for reading our stories.

Yours,
Rusty Knight and *InUPress.ca*

Dragoman Bloodgrue

Episode 023
Fourth Line Script

By Rusty Knight

Dragoman Bloodgrue
Volume V, Rulings

Previously in *Dragoman Bloodgrue* on **Summer 74 Raccoon**:

Bloodgrue walked south to carry out an errand for Master Onar. The errand took Bloodgrue to Bareington Tailor's where Bloodgrue received a courier job before continuing with Onar's task. Finishing both of those tasks Bloodgrue made purchases of his own, haggling, but not getting all the deals he desired. Bloodgrue carried his burdens with him back to 4212 Willow Road.

Dragoman Bloodgrue
Volume V, Rulings

Dragoman Bloodgrue

By Rusty Knight

Episode Twenty-three, 'Fourth Line Script'

We continue now on…

Summer 81 Raccoon

The gods' breath howls eastward again stronger than usual, waking Bloodgrue with a rattle of 4212 Willow Road's structure. Deciding it is best to rise and prepare for his client, Bloodgrue delays longer as he enjoys the luxury of his new flannel sheets. *'Beats wool all to seven hells.'* He thinks sarcastically.

Finally, conceding necessity, he gets out of bed and using the clean chamber pot, he plans his morning. Bloodgrue decided long ago never to go to sleep until he cleans his chamber pot. It just makes for a much more pleasant sleep and rise in the morning. The job today might be shitty enough.

Dressed and ready for the day, Bloodgrue walks along Osmo Road up to the two-story stone and wood structure at 5068 Osmo Road, Lexigrapher Steirn's building. Bloodgrue sighs; he got a pretty crappy job last time. He still completed it honorably and well on time. Bloodgrue wants to maintain a decent reputation. So he isn't going to put the Lexigrapher off … still.

He enters and spots Steirn at her front desk scribing a parchment poster. Bloodgrue approaches her and in his best jal, Bloodgrue addresses the noble born woman. "Gods-grace and good fate Master Steirn. You summoned me."

He waits for her to address him.

Master Steirn finishes her line then she appraises her work. She sets down her quill.

"Gods-grace and good fate young master Bloodgrue. I did. I have two important jobs for you. You did well last time. So I will trust you with these. The first; is a simple courier job to the City Watch Post with some writs. I will inform you of the other when you return from this one. Are you up to this?"

Bloodgrue ponders this. It definitely is an upgrade from the previous work Steirn gave him and easy enough. "Yes, I will do this. You have your courier pouch ready?"

Steirn reaches over to a hook on the wall and retrieves a leather pouch. She hands it to Bloodgrue and says. "Standard distance fee applies for this."

Bloodgrue nods. "Yes, it will be eight dusters."

He accepts the pouch and straps it on his waist. Stepping outside, Bloodgrue fills his waterskin from the courtyard well. Then beginning his journey, he steps out onto the Osmo Road where he heads west.

A little over an hour after noon, Bloodgrue arrive in front of 3017 Osmo Road. The City Watch Post is actively busy at the moment, and Bloodgrue debates delaying entering. But then decides that he needs to get this over with and back to Master Steirn.

Inside, the City Watch Post is packed with folks. Bloodgrue squirms his way through the crowd to the day desk. Finding day-watch Sergeant Lamcast on duty, Bloodgrue addresses him. "Sergeant Lamcast gods-grace and good fate, I have a delivery for the post, from Lexigrapher Steirn. I need a receiver and a mark."

Lamcast finishes up with the couple at his desk then he holds off the next applicant. "Dragoman Bloodgrue, are you doing courier today? Okay, I'll take it, where do you want my mark?"

Bloodgrue un-straps the pouch and takes out the receipt with the carbon stick. He hands the pouch to Lamcast for inspection and sets the parchment on the desk with the carbon stick.

Sergeant Lamcast takes the four writs out of the pouch and reads them. Then places his mark upon the sheet and says. "Thank you Bloodgrue."

Securing the receipt and the carbon stick, Bloodgrue heads back out to the street.

Walking slowly back to 5068 Osmo Road, Bloodgrue ponders what the next job might be? Is it another courier job, or something menial?

Entering the business, Bloodgrue finds Stern busy with a client. He waits for them to finish.

Approaching Steirn after her client has left; Bloodgrue offers her the courier pouch.

She looks at the mark on the receipt and smiles.

Putting these away, Steirn then addresses Bloodgrue. "The next job is of a serious nature. I need to know I can trust the person I am sending on this one. It is death to any jal except you I hear. Normally I would have to find and send a toy mercenary group in with this and not be guaranteed any results. But I heard something that tells me I will get more then a guarantee if I send you, a jal of all people, in on this. It is a trial case, Blood. A thief was caught and needs to stand trial. She asked to be tried in her home ward and the victim agreed as did the local magistrate. So I was asked to arrange it all. You are my ticket to the solution. In fact, you are more than my ticket. You are my solution. Is there any truth to you going into Western Madison and coming out?"

Bloodgrue balks momentarily on hearing all this. This sounds official. Way above his status or class out here, in this community. But he won't lie to a lexigrapher or anyone. Not directly anyway. "I have been in, and I stand here with you now."

She smiles. "That was an indirect yes. Okay. Are you capable with that sailor's sword you're wearing? And yes, I know the origin of the sword; I am a trained docks sailor as well as a lexigrapher."

Bloodgrue almost stepped back, not sure what he is being set up for truly. "I have training. I have never actually used it in combat."

Steirn's smile brightens more. "Bloodgrue, do you know the court system in Western Madison?"

Bloodgrue wonders how to carefully answer this. Then throws caution to the wind. "I am second judge on the First Justice Court. You want a trial? I'll get it in motion and carried through."

It's Steirn's turn to show disbelief or uncertainty. "Are you serious? You let me rattle on like this and you're a damn judge in there?"

Bloodgrue turns on his grin, seeing he flustered the lexigrapher, "Yes." is his simple answer.

Steirn stands and bows, then extends her arm. "Gods-grace and good fate your honor, may I request a court session?"

Bloodgrue clasps arms and answers her. "I will accept. We can try and see to it tomorrow."

Again, he is flustering Steirn. "I'm sure it doesn't need to be so quick. But it would be appreciated. Court costs will be covered by Teptun ward of course. The defendant is ready for transfer. Can you see to her transfer?"

Bloodgrue thinks a moment. He asks Steirn. "Is she mobile and safe to transfer?"

Steirn nods while answering. "Yes, she is."

Bloodgrue nods confirmation. "I will pick her up in the morning for transfer directly to the court. Court costs are ten dusters, upon pick up for transfer. All documents are to be in toydon third line script. Agreed?"

Steirn looks at Bloodgrue in disbelief. Then slowly she confirms her thoughts. "You … you're serious."

Bloodgrue nods. "Yes I am."

They clasp arms again.

Bloodgrue walks home to 4212 Willow Road.

Arriving home Bloodgrue enters the kitchen. He starts cooking evening meal.

Onar sits down to eat and Bloodgrue presents the meal.

Onar says. "Much improved apprentice, now if taste has improved as much as appearance, you are on your way to being able to say you can cook."

He tastes the tubers and smiles as Bloodgrue stands waiting. "Yes, improved, I now accept you can cook. You look like you have news and I see eight dusters on my desk this evening. Speak up."

Bloodgrue grins. "I will be away for two days Master. I have a one-day job but it may take a day to return. I leave in the morning."

Onar nods. "Good work. Keep it up Bloodgrue."

Summer 82 Raccoon

Waking up comfortable a second morning in a row, Bloodgrue doesn't want to get out of bed. Then he recalls he has the job. Jumping out of bed, Bloodgrue cleans up the best he can and puts on his Western Madison clothes, made by Guilda.

Quickly eating, he gets out on the road to Lexigrapher Steirn's later than he normally would.

The gods are breathing stronger and cold today, making exertion more comfortable, so Bloodgrue is still fresh when he arrives at 5068 Osmo Road. Entering, he wonders if he should apologize for being tardy. But he decides to refrain from doing so.

Bloodgrue greets Lexigrapher Steirn at almost noon. "Gods-grace and good fate Master Steirn, is the defendant ready to travel?"

Sitting at the desk is a roughly thirty-year-old toyfem.

The jalfem Lexigrapher sternly answers. "This is her, Master Bloodgrue. Keep her in custody and make sure she sees trial. I want to know the verdict and sentence when all is done. Here is your pouch as requested. Ten dusters and the writs from witnesses and the court transcripts are in toy third line script for you."

Bloodgrue accepts the courier pouch, opening it he inspects the contents, quickly glancing over the parchments. Roughly counting the copper coins, he seals it up and straps it in place with his pouches.

Taking the defendant by the elbow, he asks. "What is the name and case?" as he guides her to standing.

Steirn answers the question. "Her name is Rosemal; she was caught stealing from a food vender in Lesser Square. More than two Flairs value of spices and herbs."

Bloodgrue nods as he starts guiding Rosemal to the door. "Our time is short. We march now. You follow my instruction. I know the use of this shortsword, but would prefer not to use it. I do not want to have to pursue you. If I do, when you go to court I will ask for maximum sentence."

Rosemal talks while walking, answering in toy. "I know who you are. You're a judge on First Justice Court of Western Madison.

You're fair and honest. You won't have trouble from me Master Bloodgrue."

Bloodgrue sighs inwardly, thankful for even the small measures.

They arrive at the intersection of Oak Street and Fifth Avenue. Bloodgrue leads the fifteen paces out and the two stop. His hands exposed and free, he calls out loudly. "Honey, I'm Home. Where's the ale?"

Wondering how long they will have to wait, Bloodgrue is overjoyed when less than a minute later two toyfem Wardens come out to acknowledge them.

Bloodgrue address the women. "I am on business of the First Justice Court of Western Madison. This is the case charge Rosemal, under my care."

The younger toyfem turns to Rosemal. "Do you confirm?"

Bloodgrue gets nervous at that, but Rosemal quickly answers. "Yes, I do."

"You may proceed forward Blood and Rose." says the older Warden.

The two travelers walk Fifth Avenue to Red Square, quickly arriving. Entering they find it slightly crowded, with Noah busy at his table. As soon as Noah spots Bloodgrue walking towards his table, he chases away the rabble and stands to greet Bloodgrue with a hug and arm clasp.

After the greeting, Bloodgrue frowns and says. "Well, have you beaten any jalnoric tradesmen lately, dog meat?"

Noah laughs heartily and then replies. "Are you volunteering?"

Bloodgrue waves off the request, then makes his own request. "Noah, we need to call the third sitting of the Justice Court to order today. I have the defendant with me, Rosemal, and the court papers. If we can take care of this in one sitting today, I would appreciate it, so would Rosemal and Teptun Courts. We are doing this on behalf of Teptun ward."

Noah ponders this and nods. "We will do it right now. I just need to get at least one councilman as witness and one Guildsman. I'll send runners out."

Noah waves in four youths and the enforcers. He talks to them. One enforcer and the four youths scatter out the front of Red Square.

An hour passes and two ward councillors and three guildsmen arrive, with the return of the Enforcer and four youths.

The court is set up. Bloodgrue and Noah had gone over the supplied documents while they waited. They held Rosemal in room three with them as they read the documents.

Sitting at the table, they are ready.

Bloodgrue stands, drawing the now fully crowded bar crowd's attention. "Hey all, we are bringing open the third sitting of the First Justice Court of Western Madison. We have one case. Merchant Melcamp of Stall 12, in Lesser Square of Teptun ward accuses Rosemal of Western Madison, with no fixed address, of theft of over two Flairs worth of spices and herbs from his displays. We will hear from written records of the court and City Watch for the accuser, then ask Rosemal questions. After hearing her answers, Noah and I will discuss this then render our verdict and sentence. Please keep calm."

A hush closes over the room.

Bloodgrue lifts the sheaf of parchment. "The accusation states, Merchant Melcamp observed Rosemal pick up and put into a sack, inside her cloak, three satchels of saffron and two of rosemary, also two of thyme. He also observed her lift and place, a satchel of pepper into another belt pouch on her person. Apprehending her and sending another witness for a City Watch, he asked to have her searched, stating his accusations. The City Watch private searched Rosemal and found in addition to these, five pounds of salt and two satchels of rose hips. These were taken from Rosemal, as she could not say where she purchased them from. Rosemal asked that her court be held in Western Madison. The magistrate and Master Melcamp both agreed. Thus, here we are."

A hush still stands strong. Noah motions for Rosemal to stand forward for questioning. "First, how do you plead Rosemal?"

The toyfem looks sadly at Noah then Bloodgrue. "Guilty, my Lords."

Bloodgrue frustrated, asks her. "Do you have an explanation for your action?"

Rosemal nods affirmative. "I was going to sell them, to make coin to give to my family so they can feed themselves."

Bloodgrue looks at Noah, raising an eyebrow. Noah shakes his head.

Bloodgrue turns to the open court. "Thank you. We will retire and be back shortly."

The two judges enter room three, closing the door once inside.

Bloodgrue frowns frustrated. "I know the plight of poverty in here. I will give my ten dusters to her family. But we have to render guilty charge to Rosemal. What sentence though? If we take her hand, it will simply make it worse, turning her into a beggar, if she can survive."

Noah, looking out the window asks cautiously. "How about the goal? How much time can we give her?"

Bloodgrue ponders his lessons. "Law generally allows ten days to thirty years."

Noah sighs. "Say, thirty days?"

Bloodgrue thinks a bit. Then he sighs. "How about twenty days. I go back to my employer, get Merchant Melcamp, one Flair in compensation. But Rosemal has to work thirty days' wage free for the Court Magistrate?"

"I like that better." Noah responds. The two clasp arms.

Bloodgrue utters as he is opening the door. "You deliver."

Both stand at their table in front of a hushed crowd. Noah firmly delivers the response. "We find Rosemal guilt of theft. As sentence, she will go from here to the ward goal for twenty days. Upon completion of her time in the goal she will go to the Teptun Magistrate and work wage free for thirty days. Bloodgrue has ten dusters to award to Rosemal's family as compensation for loss of income. The coins are from this court."

A cheer rushes through the court. Relief washes over Rosemal. She gets to keep her hands and her sentence time is light. She moves to the judges and offers her arm to clasp.

Bloodgrue clasps first then Noah.

The two enforcers take up position, one on each side of Rosemal. With the two ward councillors, taking the lead, they march Rosemal out to the goals.

Bloodgrue turns to Noah. "My time is tight. I must be going, dog meat."

Noah stands. "I'll walk you out."

Bloodgrue empties the ten dusters onto the table and then hands them to the guildie, "Make sure her family gets all ten."

Together Noah and Bloodgrue walk Fifth Avenue up north, to Oak Street.

The gods are about to set as they reach the intersection. The two friends embrace in a hug, then clasp arms, saying their goodbyes.

Bloodgrue walks home to 4212 Willow Road, he arrives an-hour-and-a-half after mid-night.

Bloodgrue quickly gets ready and goes to sleep.

Summer 83 Raccoon

The cold wakes Bloodgrue early. He gets out of his warm bed as there is unfinished business to attend to. Planning his day, on his chamber pot, Bloodgrue is quick.

Walking to 5068 Osmo Road in record time, Bloodgrue enters the establishment shivering.

Seeing Steirn, he approaches her and sets the courier pouch on the desk. "Gods-grace and good fate Master Steirn. The deed is complete. Master Rosemal has been tried and sentenced. She was convicted of theft and sentenced to twenty days in Western Madison's goal. Plus, she must work for Teptun Magistrate, wage free for thirty days. You said the Magistrate would pay any court costs. We determined that Merchant Melcamp is due one Flair, paid by the Magistrate; this is why Rosemal will work wage free for the Magistrate. If she does not do the work to the satisfaction of the Magistrate, it will be reported to me. Agreed?"

Steirn looks at the document Bloodgrue and Noah had drawn up and nods. "Yes, of course. In exchange for your speed and concise service to me Dragoman Bloodgrue, I offer my services. Perhaps fourth line toydon script; say twenty days' worth of lessons?"

Bloodgrue halts, now stunned, blinking at his fortune. Then he nods in agreement. "Yes, agreed. But that is at least ten Flairs worth of service, are you sure?"

Steirn nods back in turn and stands, extending her arm. "Of course, what you just did would have cost me at least twenty-five Flairs; I can at least do this for you. The Flair to the merchant I will cover as well. We won't bother the Magistrate, but she will receive the work. That is fair enough by me."

Bloodgrue beams his grin and clasps arms, having made a new contact and patron.

To be continued …

In the next episode 024: '*Sir Trantor & Squire*':

Traveling to Teptun Square & Market Bloodgrue meets up with Blue Hair and she introduces him to a reluctant noble customer. Taking the reluctant noble woman to her destination, Bloodgrue receives a reward beyond any he could have expected. He returns home with a contract for another of his clients.

Awesome! You finished episode 023 of '*Dragoman Bloodgrue*'.

Let us know what you think of it by following this link: www.inupress.ca While you are there, you can join the Inevitable Unicorn Press e-mail subscription list to receive news and updates about work from our authors such as; *Rusty Knight*, Brian Hill and Aria. When you sign up for the e-mail list, you will receive a free pdf. This free pdf changes with time. Earlier the gift was a copy of *Rusty Knight's* biography of the protagonists, the Black Swans, from his novel, '*Laret*'. Later in 2016, the bonus was an episode from the serial series, '*Lanis*'.

While on the home page of InUPress.ca leave a comment, telling us what you think of our author's work or your thoughts about the website. We appreciate your time and we will respond to questions and comments.

Thank you for reading.
Yours,
Rusty Knight of Inevitable Unicorn Press.
www.inupress.ca

Dragoman
Bloodgrue

Episode 024
Sir Trantor & Squire

By Rusty Knight

Dragoman Bloodgrue
Volume V, Rulings

Welcome to our serial stories!

If you're not familiar with serials, think of them as a favorite nighttime program that continues with a new episode, only this is in print format. These are stories that don't necessarily have an end planned for them, or if they do, it's a long way off unlike many television series that we get interested in, only to have them go off air.

Serial stories are a great way to keep you entertained and on edge waiting to see what will happen next, in short enough episodes to enjoy on a lunch break, or before going to bed. Although our stories are designed to be read one episode at a time, unlike TV stories, if you just can't wait for the next episode, you can get another one any time.

Be sure to download your purchase!

It is a good idea to download the episode when you first purchase them. Then, read them at your leisure.

Please feel free to let us know what you think of our serial stories. It's a trend that may take some getting used to, but we've had positive feedback in the past with them.

Now, it's time to enjoy!
From *InUPress*,

We would like to acknowledge the following for their work in the production of this series.

Our author is, *Rusty Knight*
Our cover designer is, *Rusty Knight*
Our editing is by, Donna Shumaker (Aria)
Production and publishing is by Inevitable Unicorn Press

We at *InUPress*,
Thank you for reading *Dragoman Bloodgrue*

Dragoman Bloodgrue
Volume V, Rulings

Previously in *Dragoman Bloodgrue* on **Summer 81 Raccoon**:

Summoned by Lexigrapher Steirn, Bloodgrue feared a menial job fit for a low class. But he ended up with a courier job delivering writs to the City Watch post on Osmo Road. Returning the courier pouch to Steirn, Bloodgrue was rewarded with another job escorting a criminal into Western Madison to stand trial, where Bloodgrue stands as judge. Carrying out the trial, Bloodgrue then informed Steirn of the results. Steirn then rewarded Bloodgrue with twenty days of fourth line script lessons

Dragoman Bloodgrue

By Rusty Knight

Episode twenty-four, 'Sir Trantor & Squire'

We continue now on …

Summer 84 Raccoon

Bloodgrue is preparing Onar's morning meal when he hears knocking on the business door. It is gods-rise, early for most clients, but Bloodgrue feels obligated to answer. He removes all food from the flames so it doesn't burn and proceeds to answer the door.

At the door there are six people milling about outside. A toymal of about thirty-five-years age addresses Bloodgrue in toy. "Gods-grace and good fate Dragoman Bloodgrue, we seek to ask favours from you."

Bloodgrue nods and he gestures for the six people to enter the common room.

They enter solemnly. The man continues. "My name is Malak; this is Joseph, Masala, Angernon, Jered and Larsmal." He says as he points to a twenty-fivish jalmal, then a teenage jalfem, a twenty-fivish toymal, a thirtyish jalmal and finally a teenage toymal.

Malak bows and continues to speak in toy. "We seek your aid, Master Bloodgrue, as we know you have done favours for others and done them well. May we speak?"

Bloodgrue ponders this. His name is spreading as a person who helps others, even though his influence has only been with a few. But it doesn't hurt; he now has a modest income from helping others. "Yes, go ahead."

The group sighs together.

Malak speaks for them again. "We are seeking work and wondered if you could help us find employment."

Bloodgrue, stunned, as he can count on one hand those he helped find employment. But he does hear from some who look for workers. So he decides. "I will help. But it will be the same deal as the others. One duster now, to take up your search and five percent of your income when I find you work."

The group huddles together then four of the members' approach Bloodgrue.

First up is the twenty-five-year-old jalmal. "My name is Joseph, of 3612 Caraway Avenue. I am a Labourer, I'll work anywhere." He deftly hands Bloodgrue a duster.

Second up is the thirtyish jalmal. "My name is Jered, of number 24, 3617 Trouft House, Caraway Avenue. I am a Labourer; I too will work anywhere." He offers Bloodgrue a duster.

Third up is the twenty-fivish toymal. "My name is Angernon. I am from number sixteen 3617 Trouft House on Caraway Avenue. I am a labourer and I only work in Trenton ward, Master Bloodgrue. I have family to tend too daily." He cautiously hands Bloodgrue a duster.

The last to consult with Bloodgrue is the toymal teenager. "Gods-grace and good fate dragoman, my name is Larsmal. I live at number thirty-two 3617 Trouft House on Caraway Avenue. I have no skills but I'll learn anything. I'll work damn near anywhere, even if I have to move." He eagerly offers Bloodgrue a duster.

Bloodgrue memorizes the four names and takes all four dusters. Labourers are easier to get work in some areas, harder in others. Angernon will be difficult to place. The easiest will be Larsmal.

"Okay folks, I will do what I can for you all. I will find you when I find you work. I will get you a most favourable contract when I get you one. It will benefit both of us." Bloodgrue ushers out the six. Now four dusters richer and with four contracts to fill, he clasps arms with each of the four as they exit.

Bloodgrue finishes preparing Onar's morning meal and serves Onar without mention of the clients.

About two hours before the noon hour, Bloodgrue leaves 4212 Willow Road and heads to Teptun Square & Market.

Bloodgrue wanders the market listening to and observing people. He gravitates to stall 74 with his mentor and patron.

Blue Hair, is excited again to see Bloodgrue, as she has a young woman with her. "Bloodgrue, get the Seven Hells over here. Gods-grace good fate boy … About time someone trustworthy showed up. I have been trying to explain to Esmelda here how to get to Tant Manor – instead, now she is going to hire you to escort her to her new posting there."

Bloodgrue walks close to Blue Hair and laughing clasps arms with her. Deciding on the spot that she is his favorite patron. He should simply visit her stall first upon arriving in Teptun's. "Done Blue Hair, what is the address for Tant Manor? I don't recall the name?"

Blue Hair releases the clasp while smiling. "It's an easy one for you, boy. 106 Spider Avenue."

Bloodgrue chuckles heartily. "That will be two Dyns Master Esmelda. It's a day and a half walk. We can start now. Do you have baggage or companions?"

Esmelda frowns. "You're rude to be talking to me so. I'm a squire to a Baron. My pampamoo is a Baron. You better address me properly boy."

Bloodgrue hesitates. In this class ridden society she is right; he could be flogged for talking so lightly to her. But in his defense, he hadn't been informed she was a noble, and she doesn't show rank. "My apologies Sir Esmelda, I was unaware you are a squire of noble birth. I ask forgiveness. My questions stand though. Do you have baggage or companions traveling with you? Sir Esmelda."

The squire seems more at ease now and addresses Bloodgrue. "Dragoman, I have no baggage or companions. My pampamoo saw fit to send me to my new posting with only what I wear. We can start our journey now."

Bloodgrue has an idea. "Sir Esmelda, are you hungry or thirsty?"

The squire perks up slightly at this. "Somewhat, yes."

Bloodgrue un-slings his pack and takes out one of his fresher pieces of hard tack and offers it to Esmelda.

Esmelda eagerly accepts the food and begins eating, as Bloodgrue places his pack back in place.

Then Bloodgrue starts walking, he offers her one of his two waterskins of dark ale.

The squire enjoys a few sips of ale to chase the hard tack and this seems to lighten her mood considerably.

They walk Spider Avenue until nearly gods-set, when Bloodgrue takes them into a bed and breakfast called Morelot.

Talking with the proprietor, an eighty-five-year-old jalfem name Anna, Bloodgrue gets two rooms with breakfast, for one Dyns each.

Summer 85 Raccoon

Gods-rise and the two are on the avenue walking again. The scattered cover in the sphere seems to be holding the heat low on the ground and it is uncomfortable walking in, even with the west breath of the gods.

Half-an-hour before noon they arrive at the gates to the courtyard of Tant Manor. 106 Spider Avenue is a manor estate of approximately 1,400 acres.

Entering the estate, the two find the manor house to be a three story, field stone structure of good looking condition.

Bloodgrue leads the way to the front double doors. He addresses a cleanly liveried toymal teenager. "Excuse me please; I bring Squire Esmelda to her post with Sir Trantor. Where will we find Sir Trantor?"

The boy looks at Esmelda, then opening the door he gestures for the two to follow. He leads them into a hall where an elderly jalmal is eating mid-day meal alone.

The boy says to the elderly man. "Sir Trantor you have guests."

The boy quickly leaves.

Sir Trantor nods and views Bloodgrue and Esmelda.

Pointing to Bloodgrue, Trantor says. "Speak up boy."

Bloodgrue bows and says, "I am Apprentice Dragoman Bloodgrue, presenting your squire Esmelda from Baron Terrent, Sir Trantor."

Trantor beam and shout loudly. "Escarot, two more sets for mid-day."

Then less loudly and pointing first to his left then to his right at the seats. "Bloodgrue, you sit there. Squire, you there."

Trantor is smiling as he addresses them both. "I don't get much company here, so Bloodgrue, I would appreciate you being my guest tonight."

Bloodgrue, never having been a guest at a noble's table or manor before is uncomfortable, but he sees an opportunity. "Of course, I would be most honored and I will collect my fees when I leave, Sir Trantor."

Trantor looks at Bloodgrue humorously. "Don't be silly, let's get that dealt with now. How much dragoman?"

Bloodgrue, deciding to get it dealt with quickly as well, answers. "The dragoman fee is two Dyns, plus two Dyns for food and lodging. So four Dyns, Sir Trantor."

Sir Trantor takes four Dyns from his pouch and pays Bloodgrue. Bloodgrue puts the coins in his pouch.

The servant sets plates of food in front of Esmelda and Bloodgrue. On the plate is pheasant and boiled tubers, along with beans and spiced rice. Also added to the meal are bread and cheese with a tankard of mead and a tumbler of milk.

Sir Trantor looks at each guest then shrugging he smiles. He then says, "I have to give Esmelda basic lessons and you might benefit dragoman. I want to get this out of the way today, so Esmelda can get to real squire training. So, you can ask questions if you want. But here goes the basics."

Trantor takes a drink of his mead then starts the lesson. "The basics of nobility is pretty simple in the Dominnion of Kannoral. At the top we have the Royal, this can either be a King or Queen, doesn't really matter which. Under the Royal is the Earl, called either a Lady or Lord. Now the Earl has an Earldom which he holds, which is an entire district or Shireward. They are districts, if inside the cities of Mount Oryn or Dendar. They are Shirewards outside the two cities. Answering to the Royal and Earls, are Barons, Knights and Bailiffs. Also there are the various trades, crafts and guilds. Earls hold Shire Hall Moots which are judicial courts. A Baron holds either one or two manors or fiefs, directly or through a vassal Knight or Bailiff. A Baron can hold a judicial moot hall for his holdings. Knight-commanders hold a manor of fief, while a Knight-bachelor has no holding. A Bailiff directs a fief or manor for a Knight, Baron, Earl or Royal, and occasionally for a guild. Now the titles are hereditary but can also be conferred by a Royal. Then there are the guilds, tradesmen and craftsmen, followed by apprentices, then freemen and farmers. Below these are the commoners and villeins, then labourers followed by serfs and un-free, indentured and peasants. Last are slaves, beggars, then prisoners. That is the basics, if broken into the class system; it is of upper-class, middle-class and lower-class. Of the upper-class, there are the upper-upper-class, the Royal, middle-upper-class the Earls and Barons and Arch-bishops and Bishops, the lower-upper-class they are the knights and deacons. There are the middle class. There are the upper-middle-class which is the guild, trades and crafts, masters, some squires are considered upper-middle-class if they are vassals of knight-bachelors. The middle-middle-class are the trades, crafts and guilds, journeymen, priests, as well as some explorers and adventuring types who can economically afford to support the life. The lower-middle-class is apprentices, freemen and farmers. Then there is the lower Class. The upper-lower-class is commoners, labourers and villeins. The middle-lower-class is serfs, un-free, peasants and the indentured. The lowest life forms are the lower-lower-class, slaves, beggars and prisoners. So there you have our society in a hand basket."

Trantor looks at both of his entranced students. "Any questions so far?"

Both shake their heads no.

Trantor sighs but smiles.

"Okay then a second lesson. Heraldry in the Dominnion of Kannoral is exercised by rights conferred by the Officer of Arms. There are two basic shapes, the shield and the lozenge. The face of either is the field. Blazoning of the Coat of Arms is describing the arms in formal language, a description of the shield and crest with supporters, motto and other insignia, using the rules of tincture and such, applying physical and artistic description to the nature and form. The left side of our coat of arms is the dextor, while the right side is sinistor. Supporters are the human or animal figures on the sides supporting the shield. The motto is the phrase or collection of words we use to describe the motivation or intention of the holder of the coat of arms. Once chosen it is set. Sometimes, multiple coats of arms are placed in a field to express combining an occupation of office or inheritance, this is called marshaling. When heraldic badges are placed on a flag that is elongated and pointed or swallow tail that flag is a pennon. A square flag we use, that is charged with the full coat of arms, is a Banner of Arms and they are of set size depending on noble rank. For example, the king's is four and a half feet square, while a baron's is only three feet square. A standard is a tapered heraldic display flag starting at four feet in height, tapering down to two feet in height. The field is two colours to display the owners rank and livery colours, with his motto, displaying heraldic badges of those under his charge. The length varies by the noble's rank. The king's is twenty-one feet long while a guild can bear one only six feet long. A baron's is ten feet long."

The now awed, Bloodgrue and an inspired Esmelda have both had a lesson, teaching them some basics of Kannoral noble knowledge.

Bloodgrue has been granted knowledge shared with only the small few in the noble class.

Sir Trantor goes on to teach them more on manors, fiefs and economics of the noble class. Spending the entire evening in study, Bloodgrue gains more respect and appreciation for the difficulty of managing society.

Bloodgrue gains knowledge he can use in his progress through his status.

As evening closes Bloodgrue proposes the hiring of the four labourers.

Sir Trantor agrees to a contract with Jered for three dusters per day starting Autumn 1 Raccoon. They draw up the contract for Jered to mark.

Summer 86 Raccoon

The contract carefully sealed in his pouch, both waterskins filled with mead and some fresh hard tack in his pack; Bloodgrue clasps arms with Sir Trantor and then Sir Esmelda, wishing them well.

At gods-rise, Bloodgrue starts for Teptun Square & Market. Bloodgrue walks at a steady but easy pace, trying to try to arrive at Teptun's today.

Bloodgrue arrives at Stall 74's usual location after evening meal time. He arrives to find Blue Hair in place with one carcass still hanging. The heat has it turning a bit, but someone's dog could still make use of it.

Bloodgrue addresses Blue Hair. "More jobs like that please, old one. I learned a lot from the Baron. He is a nice fellow and took time to teach me. I owe you two dusters."

Bloodgrue proudly hands Blue Hair two dusters.

"I have to go home and get some sleep now. I did this return in one shot today and I am going to go all the way home. Twelve hours of walking or more. See you later Blue Hair." He clasps arms with his patron then walks away.

Entering 4212 Willow Road, Bloodgrue knows Onar will be in his sitting room. In half-an-hour the gods will set. That's fourteen hours of walking today.

Finding Onar, Bloodgrue silently places two Dyns on the desk and then walks to his room, collapsing on his bed. He is almost asleep before hitting the bed, lying on top of the covers.

To be continue on …

Dragoman Bloodgrue
Volume V, Rulings

In the next episode 025, *'Duck Tavern's Emerald'*:

Bloodgrue delivers a contract of labour to Labourer Jered. Onar then has Bloodgrue deliver a courier package to Anchor's Rest and while in the ward, Bloodgrue goes to Duck Tavern where one lad dies trying to steal the Duck Emerald and a second thief who attempts to steal it barely survives.

Awesome! You finished episode 024 of '*Dragoman Bloodgrue*'.

Let us know what you think of it by following this link: www.inupress.ca While you are there, you can join the Inevitable Unicorn Press e-mail subscription list to receive news and updates about work from our authors such as; *Rusty Knight*, Brian Hill and Aria. When you sign up for the e-mail list, you will receive a free pdf. This free pdf changes with time. Earlier the gift was a copy of *Rusty Knight's* biography of the protagonists, the Black Swans, from his novel, *'Laret'*. Later in 2016, the bonus was an episode from the serial series, *'Lanis'*.

While at InUPress.ca leave a comment, telling us what you think of our author's work or your thoughts about the website. We appreciate your time and we will respond to questions and comments.

Thank you for reading.
Yours,
Rusty Knight of Inevitable Unicorn Press.
www.inupress.ca

Dragoman Bloodgrue
Episode 025
Duck Tavern's
Emerald
By Rusty Knight

Dragoman Bloodgrue
Volume V, Rulings

Welcome to our serial stories!

If you're not familiar with serials, think of them as a favorite nighttime program that continues with a new episode, only this is in print format. These are stories that don't necessarily have an end planned for them, or if they do, it's a long way off unlike many television series that we get interested in, only to have them go off air.

Serial stories are a great way to keep you entertained and on edge waiting to see what will happen next, in short enough episodes to enjoy on a lunch break, or before going to bed. Although our stories are designed to be read one episode at a time, unlike TV stories, if you just can't wait for the next episode, you can get another one any time.

Be sure to download your purchase!

It is a good idea to download the episode when you first purchase them. Then, read them at your leisure.

Please feel free to let us know what you think of our serial stories. It's a trend that may take some getting used to, but we've had positive feedback in the past with them.

Now, it's time to enjoy!
From *InUPress*,

We would like to acknowledge the following for their work in the production of this series.

Our author is, *Rusty Knight*
Our cover designer is, *Rusty Knight*
Our editing is by, Donna Shumaker (Aria)
Production and publication is by, *InUPress*

We at *InUPress*,
Thank you for reading *Dragoman Bloodgrue*

Dragoman Bloodgrue
Volume V, Rulings

Previously in *Dragoman Bloodgrue* on **Summer 84 Raccoon**:

 Going to Teptun Square & Market, Bloodgrue met up with Blue Hair and she introduced him to a reluctant noble client. Taking the reluctant Noble woman to her destination, Bloodgrue received a reward beyond any he could have expected. He returned home with a contract for another of his clients.

37

Dragoman Bloodgrue

By Rusty Knight

Episode twenty-five, 'Duck Tavern's Emerald'

We continue now on …

Summer 87 Raccoon

Bloodgrue wakes with a yawn in darkness of night. He stretches and considers his task. It's at least eight hours walking to Trouft House on Caraway Avenue.

Rising from the warm flannel sheets, Bloodgrue does his business on the chamber pot, making his days' plans. Getting dressed in his clean Onar clothes, Bloodgrue lights his candle and begins his morning chores.

"Master Onar, I'm headed to Trouft House on Caraway Avenue today, will you have work for me in that direction?" asks Bloodgrue as he serves Onar the scrambled eggs just the way his Master requested they be cooked. The two day-gods rose above the eastern horizon roughly ten minutes ago.

Onar shrugs as he observes the properly cooked eggs and diced tubers. He smiles and says to Bloodgrue. "You are getting much better at cooking. I'm becoming impressed. You're slow though, it took you six years. Go south; when you come back I want you to take a package for a client to Anchor's Rest. It goes to 1416 Yarrow Street, deliver it then see what job you can pick up down there. Don't forget the package is already paid for but if you can get a tip go ahead and collect."

Bloodgrue nods and finishes his chores. Getting ready with two waterskins and some hard tack, Bloodgrue confirms he has the contract in his pack. He sets out on his journey.

…..

It had started raining three hours ago. Bloodgrue opens the front entry to Trouft house at 3617 Caraway Avenue. Climbing the stairs, he brushes off as much of the rain as possible. On the second floor he looks for #24. Getting half way down the hall he finds the door and knocks. A second knock is needed before the thirty-three-year-old tall jalmal answers.

"Gods-grace and good fate Master Jered. It is Apprentice Dragoman Bloodgrue with news for you. May I enter?" answers a beleaguered Bloodgrue.

Jered blinks then nods. "Gods-grace and good fate, of course Master Bloodgrue, enter. Come in and tell me your news." He steps back in and to the side.

Bloodgrue steps into a small room that is about twelve feet by fifteen feet with one other exit and one window. In the room is a small warming brazier and a small table with three chairs. There is a cupboard with a basin and assorted pottery and cutlery. On the table sits a tea pot and a single cold cup of tea.

"May I have a cup of tea, Jered? It was an eight hour walk and nearly the last half was in rain." Bloodgrue states with a shiver.

Jered frowns but fetches a second cup from the cupboard and pours it full from the pot. Sitting, he sets the full cup on the table. He points to one of the chairs. "Help yourself and sit."

Bloodgrue gets the feeling he's pulling hens teeth here but he continues with his errand. Taking a seat at the table, Bloodgrue drinks some of the cold tea. Bloodgrue states. "I have work for you. It's a five-year contract with possible recurring extensions. Your pay will be three dusters per day with Sir Trantor of Tant Manor. You will pay me thirteen dusters every first day of each season starting Winter 1 Raccoon. There will be bonuses for both of us as time goes on. Do you need me to get you to Tant Manor for Autumn 1 Raccoon, which is your official start day?"

Jered stares blankly at Bloodgrue for more than a minute then he smiles and extends his arm excitedly. "By all mean, no I don't need you to guide me. You have done enough. Give me the address and I will seek it out right away dragoman."

Bloodgrue smiles and replies to Jered. "Tant Manor is at 106 Spider Avenue in Archoman ward. Do you mind if I stay the night before heading home? I'll pay a duster."

Jered frowns then counters. "I'm low on funds and food, so two dusters and you can stay the night."

Bloodgrue accepts the arm clasp and pays the two dusters. He takes the contract from his pack, handing it to Jered.

Autumn 88 Raccoon

The world was wet from the rains last night for Bloodgrue's walk. Bloodgrue arrived back at 4212 Willow road in time to cook Onar's evening meal. Then he got dagger practice in and some other lessons.

Sitting in his room Bloodgrue ponders events. He is feeling Blue Hair needs a visit after running the errand for Onar tomorrow. Time to get some sleep now. After making sure the chamber pot is clean, Bloodgrue climbs into the comfy bed and soon is lost to slumber.

Autumn 89 Raccoon

Onar was particularly mean and grumpy this morning to Bloodgrue. Smacking Bloodgrue's back for over cooking the porridge and tea.

…..

The package is about fifteen pounds as Bloodgrue carries it up to the door at 1416 Yarrow Street.

Being about noon, Bloodgrue isn't sure if the resident will be home but he knocks on the smaller two and a half story structure's wood door. Bloodgrue waits and counts … fifteen … sixteen. The door opens and a jalmal, appearing seventy years old, steps out. "Wha the seven ells yah want?"

Bloodgrue grins his broad famous grin. "Gods-grace and good fate Master Harad. I have a package for you. If you will make your mark on my ticket I will be on my way?"

The old jalmal frowns angrily. "Make it snappy. I'm busy."

Harad then makes his mark on Bloodgrue's parchment ticket and takes the package without further word. Not giving any tip, Harad closes the door on Bloodgrue.

Highly disappointed but used to such clients, Bloodgrue decides to walk to the Duck to see about drumming up a paying client. The walk is about an hour and he can refocus on the way.

Entering the Duck, Bloodgrue wonders why anyone would name a tavern the Duck. But he figures there is a story there somewhere back in the origin of the tavern.

Spotting Gena, the thirty some toyfem barmaid, Bloodgrue walks to the bar and waves her over.

"A client and dark ale please, Gena my dear." Bloodgrue states when she arrives.

Gena laughs and responds. "How about you offer me clients and two dusters?"

Bloodgrue pays Gena two dusters and she pours him a tankard of dark ale.

Bloodgrue is hanging out in the Duck without getting lucky, when he notices a young jalmal trying to pry the emerald free from the mantle over the fireplace.

Bloodgrue shouts at the male quickly. "Whoa there, stop!"

He pulls free his dagger from the waist band of his leggings and rushes towards the youth. As he does so, a thirtyish year old jalmal farmer joins Bloodgrue in defending the Duck.

As Bloodgrue reaches the youth, the young man has a dagger in hand and quickly stabs Bloodgrue in the leg.

The farmer punches the thief in the chest, knocking him back.

They move for positions, feinting back and forth.

"You need to stop! Stealing the Emerald is a bad idea. People die trying, Lad." Says Gena from the side of the conflict.

The lad says angrily. "No way, I'm not giving way! I'm leaving."

The short silent farmer sweeps out and strikes the lad's right leg, knocking him down. As the boy is recovering, Bloodgrue positions to block the possible exit.

The thief is so dazed that the farmer is able to quickly hit him again knocking him out.

This leaves Bloodgrue to use his ball of twine to tie the boy's wrists together.

Gena looks around the room and spots a young jalfem observing the incident. Gena calls to her. "Tama, go get the City Watch and a Pandora. Be quick girl. City Watch first."

The heavy set eighteen-year-old jalfem quickly exits the Duck as the boy regains his senses.

Bloodgrue and the farmer set the boy on a chair as Gena addresses him. "Boyo what's your name?"

The thief shakes his head once while blinking his eyes. "Damn seven hells all of you. I'm not telling you my name."

An older jalmal tells Gena quietly. "His name be Fotner, Master Gena."

Gena nods. "Drink on the house for you Master Gearris … Master Fotner, you have two choices right now. IN about three minutes you will likely die horribly. Or you can pay me two Dyns and I will give you a potion and help try to save your life. But still turn you over to either the City Watch or Pandora. So which is it, die or two Dyns?"

Fotner frowns but smirks. "I ain't got no two Dyns and I ain't gona die. The City Watch ain't gona do nothing. Who the seven hells is Pandora?"

There is a collective ooh from six of the gathered in the room.

Gena utters matter-of-fact. "As you wish Master Fotner, you were warned and I have seven witnesses here now. You now have about two minutes to change your mind … Sorry, less."

The time passes as Gena sits down to wait for the City Watch, after she serves Gearris a light ale.

Two minutes' pass, suddenly Fotner starts to violently convulse. His whole body wracked in waves of muscle spasms. And almost twenty seconds after that his hands burst into bright blue flames. The convulsions wrack his body violently for about thirty seconds, knocking Fotner from the chair. The flames burn the skin and flesh free from the bones of his hands in less than twenty seconds.

Gearris, in a rush, checks the boy when his body is still. He looks around in horror. "He's dead. There's no flesh left on his hands at all. Just the bones remain. No breathing at all."

Gena looks around the room and she shares with those gathered in the tavern, including two new arrivals. "Folks, this is what happens if you even try to touch that Duck Emerald. So please not even out of curiosity, do not touch it. If you try to steal it, tell me I can help you."

Almost right away a thirty-year-old appearing, taller skinny toymal, with his hands held in front of him, his eyes wide in terror red and watery, rushes to Gena. Mouth gasping for air he gasps out in broken words of toy. "I … I touch ... ed it. pl … ease help."

Gena looks at the man and hesitates then asks. "Did you try to steal the Emerald? And what is your name?"

He stutters less but gets out quickly. "Ye … es … T … Tasal."

Gena tisks sadly then stands, she looks the man over. "Two Dyns now, Tasal."

Tasal quickly takes his coin pouch off his belt and hands it to Gena. She hands it to Bloodgrue and heads to the back door, returning in less than a minute with a wash basin of water on a tray. On the tray also is a bowl with powder, a towel, and a small crystal vial of red liquid.

Bloodgrue places the two small silver coins, taken from Tasal's pouch, on the same table.

Gena offers Tasal the vial. "Drink this quickly and wash your hands afterwards. Use lots of the soap. There is a special powder in it that neutralizes the alchemical part of the curse. The potion neutralizes the main curse. If you try to run, the soap also has an ingredient that allows my mage friend to find you and we won't be bringing the City Watch with us. My friends coming with me will include Pandora enforcers. So be smart and stay after you wash your hands. Dry them off very well with the towel."

Tasal quickly drinks the vial of red liquid and after setting the vial on the table he vigorously washes his hands, judiciously using the powder to wash all the way up to his elbows. Then after rinsing off, he dries thoroughly. Almost in tears he sits in the chair. "I need it to feed my family. We haven't had work in almost a season. We need work or coin. The gem has to be worth at least a thousand Flairs. I could pay my year's taxes and a year's rent and feed my family for a year with the thousand and have coin left."

Gena sadly sighs. "If you stole the Duck Emerald and sold it for a thousand Flairs I would have to find you and kill you for gullibility or stupidity. That there gem is worth over five thousand Flairs, Tasal. But with the curse on it, its cost is your life for trying to steal it. Next time I won't save you. I normally charge a Flair and only save a person once. So don't be stupid and get the seven hells out of here now."

Bloodgrue places his hand on Tasal's arm. "Hold there one minute Tasal. We have had one victim today. Gena gave you an opportunity to live. The City Watch will be here any minute now and so will Pandora. But I help folks get work. Tell me what you do and your address. If I get you a contract, you owe me five percent of your contract every first of the season. It will cost you one duster now and seeing as I own your coin purse now, we will consider it the price of trying to steal the Duck Emerald. So your occupation and address, Tasal?"

Tasal, still in shock at the event and then hearing the value of the Emerald, hesitates then answers Bloodgrue in rapid fire. "Journeymen Woodworker, 416 Yeman Street, Anchor's Rest."

Bloodgrue still has a hold of Tasal's arm. Bloodgrue looks puzzled, he asks in curiosity. "If you're a journeyman woodworker why are you out of work?"

Tasal looks at Bloodgrue. "My son took to bloodfires. With the cost of the physician I had to sell my tools to pay her. My son lives but I have no shop or tools."

Bloodgrue's mind ticks over in three or four cycles and he asks eagerly. "So if I could get you set up with tools or in a shop you could be working again?"

Tasal nods eagerly. "Yes, but that's not easy as it would cost many Flairs or a willing master."

Bloodgrue nods again, his mind actively searching for master woodworkers he knows. He has some visiting to do as Blood of First Rank. "Master Tasal, I am keeping your pouch but I am going to take up your cause as well. You are not forgotten or alone. If I can at least set it up so you get tools, where can you work? Do you have a shop you can work in?"

Tasal thinks a moment. "There is a shop I can rent. It is five Flairs a season."

Bloodgrue releases his arm and gestures towards the doorway. "Go."

Looking down at his leg wound, Bloodgrue asks Gena. "Is it safe to use this water to wash my wound to avoid bloodfires?"

Gena nods slowly and smiles. "I will get fresh water if you split the pouch fifty-fifty."

Bloodgrue nods happily. "Done and I'll buy another dark ale too."

Gena removes the tray of used items.

Bloodgrue exposes the leg wound and Gena returns with a basin of clean warm water and a clean towel, as well as fresh soap powder. Bloodgrue grimaces as he washes the wound, finding it stings greatly.

Gena serves him a tankard of dark ale.

The patrons are confused as these two seem to carry on free willed, unconcern with a corpse at their feet.

Legging and dagger back in place, with the dagger wound clean, Bloodgrue divvies up the coins from Tasal's coin pouch. It amounts to Gena getting one Flair, one Dyns and four dusters, as does Bloodgrue.

Dragoman Bloodgrue
Volume V, Rulings

Almost half-an-hour after Tama left, the first City Watch arrives. Two City Watch privates enter as Gena gets rid of Tasal's coin pouch.

To be continued …

In the next episode 026, *'Blue Hair's Shortsword'*:

Bloodgrue seeks out Blue Hair for lessons in shortsword use. But finds other lessons he wasn't bargaining for.

Awesome! You finished episode 025 of '*Dragoman Bloodgrue*'.

Let us know what you think of it by following this link: www.inupress.ca While you are there, you can join the Inevitable Unicorn Press e-mail subscription list to receive news and updates about work from our authors such as; *Rusty Knight*, Brian Hill and Aria. When you sign up for the e-mail list, you will receive a free pdf. This free pdf changes with time. Earlier the gift was a copy of *Rusty Knight's* biography of the protagonists, the Black Swans, from his novel, '*Laret*'. Later in 2016, the bonus was an episode from the serial series, '*Lanis*'.

While at InUPress.ca leave a comment, telling us what you think of our author's work or your thoughts about the website. We appreciate your time and we will respond to questions and comments.

Thank you for reading.
Yours,
Rusty Knight of Inevitable Unicorn Press.
www.inupress.ca

Dragoman Bloodgrue
Episode 026
Blue Hair's
Shortsword
By Rusty Knight

Dragoman Bloodgrue
Volume V, Rulings

Welcome to our serial stories!

If you're not familiar with serials, think of them as a favorite nighttime program that continues with a new episode, only this is in print format. These are stories that don't necessarily have an end planned for them, or if they do, it's a long way off unlike many television series that we get interested in, only to have them go off air.

Serial stories are a great way to keep you entertained and on edge waiting to see what will happen next, in short enough episodes to enjoy on a lunch break, or before going to bed. Although our stories are designed to be read one episode at a time, unlike TV stories, if you just can't wait for the next episode, you can get another one any time.

Be sure to download your purchase!

It is a good idea to download the episode when you first purchase them. Then, read them at your leisure.

Please feel free to let us know what you think of our serial stories. It's a trend that may take some getting used to, but we've had positive feedback in the past with them.

Now, it's time to enjoy!
From *InUPress*,

We would like to acknowledge the following for their work in the production of this series.

The author is *Rusty Knight*
Our cover designer is, *Rusty Knight*
Our editing is by, Donna Shumaker (Aria)
Production and publication is by, *InUPress*

We at *InUPress*,
Thank you for reading *Dragoman Bloodgrue*

Dragoman Bloodgrue
Volume V, Rulings

Previously in *Dragoman Bloodgrue* on **Summer 87 Raccoon**:

Bloodgrue delivered a contract of labour to Labourer Jered. Onar then had Bloodgrue deliver a courier package to Anchor's Rest and while in the ward, Bloodgrue went to Duck tavern where one lad died trying to steal the Duck Emerald and a second thief who attempted to steal the emerald, barely survived.

Dragoman Bloodgrue
Volume V, Rulings

Dragoman Bloodgrue

By Rusty Knight

Episode twenty-six, 'Blue Hair's Shortsword'

We continue now on …

Summer 89 Raccoon

Private Hatford addresses Gena as if bored. "So what's the issue you summoned the Watch for?"

Gena points to the corpse of Fotner and replies dejected. "Add another unfortunate body to the list of thieves trying to steal my Emerald. Private Hatford, I am reporting the attempted theft, and the death by the curse, as a result. When will they learn not to touch the cursed thing?"

Hatford looks around the tavern. "Anyone here confirm this?"

Bloodgrue and three patrons raise their hands slowly.

Hatford walks over to the dead boy and kicks him hard twice, slightly jolting the body that is stiffening already. "You really should remove that cursed gem, Gena. You rack up at least one corpse a season. And we're not removing them anymore. It's your responsibility. You deal with the dead and their families. We're done, just report it. The report cost you one Flair for our time and effort. Pay now."

Gena looks at Private Hatford in mock shock; actually she has been expecting this for two seasons now. Reaching into her coin pouch, Gena pulls out a Flair and she hands it respectfully to Private Hatford. The middle-aged jalfem officer accepts the coin and motions to her toymal partner, Private Mesmar, and the two humans exit the Duck.

Gena sighs and she looks at Bloodgrue saying sarcastically. "Well he at least paid for his own expenses so far. How much to disposes of him, now?"

Looking around at the patrons, Gena sees that Tama is back again. "Tama, next drink is on the house if you fetch a local priest of Stonewire quickly. I am thinking this boy is going stiff on me already."

Tama stands and hurriedly leaves the Duck.

Bloodgrue frowns bitterly. "One a season? Really? Why not get rid of the emerald?"

Gena frowns, seeming upset at the silliness of the question. "Really? You see what happens when someone touches the beast. The Duck Emerald is cursed and it's not an alchemical curse. It is an actual contact curse and you can wear gloves all you want. Touching the beast brings on the curse. My brother died finding that gem. I lost a friend when they mounted it there. It took three years to discover the cure and neutralization for the curse and twenty thousand Flairs that my adventuring friends put up for the research. No! … It stays and stupid people can keep trying to steal it. The neutralization only works once and only for an hour … so handling the Duck Emerald after an hour invites the curse again. Bloodgrue, it stays there so I know where it's at."

Bloodgrue places two dusters on the table and Gena serves him a dark ale. She then continues to serve her customers.

A short time later an eighty or so years old jalfem in the garb of a high ranking Priest of Stonewire arrives with Tama.

Gena serves Tama a light ale then approaches the Priestess. "Gods-grace and good fate Priestess Haudmal. It's been a while; I am saddened to inform you I have a new corpse just ripe for Stonewire's plane."

The old jalfem nods sagely and looks Gena in the eyes. "Show me the corpse and spare the rhetoric, heathen."

Gena barely blinks as she leads Haudmal to Fotner's corpse.

Haudmal extends her hand slowly, palm up.

"The fee for dispersal is eight Dyns for this corpse and two able bodied living for transporting him."

Gena coughs softly as now this is actually coming from her funds not from Fotner. She hands Haudmal eight Dyns then looks around the room.

Haudmal points out two toymals and waves them over. "We have work for you. It's worth two dusters for two hours of your time. Gena will give you an ale, on the house, when you return here." Haudmal utters firmly as she looks at the two human males.

Gena doesn't protest and the two toydon males agree. Toymal being stockier shorter humans tend to do more of the labour work.

Haudmal motions for them to carry Fotner and to follow her.

The body gone and dealt with, Bloodgrue sees it's time to move on and leaves the Duck.

Arriving at Teptun Square & Market as the two day-gods are touching the peaks of the tallest buildings on the west side, Bloodgrue is not surprised to find Blue Hair is not at her spot at stall 74. He decides to walk home tonight.

Arriving home around mid-night, Bloodgrue quickly cleans up and places one Dyns on Onar's desk.

Summer 90 Raccoon

Waking an-hour-and-a-half, or more, before the two day-gods break over the eastern horizon, Bloodgrue quickly grooms and cleans his small eight foot by eight-foot room. Making his bed and emptying his chamber pot he is ready.

Leaving 4212 Willow Road long before Onar rises from his rooms, Bloodgrue makes good time along Willow Road then west along Osmo Road until the intersection with Elmar Road East. Following the twists and turns of Elmar Road East, Bloodgrue arrives in the northern section of Teptun Square & Market. Bloodgrue chose to avoid the east entrance today as the north entrance alleyway has a more direct line to the fountain and thus more direct to stall 74, Blue Hair's chicken butcher stall.

Even being direct, it is almost a kilometre through stalls and shops to the centre of the market and to stall 74.

Bloodgrue arrives at stall 74 finding Blue Hair busy with a jalfem customer. Doing a quick mental note that Blue Hair has two carcasses left, Bloodgrue hangs around the area waiting for the customer to finish. She takes nearly three-quarters-of-an-hour.

Bloodgrue is ready and swoops in.

"I'd like to buy one of these fine chickens for one Flair, Master Blue Hair." offers an eager Bloodgrue.

Blue Hair is used to excited clients, but is curious why Bloodgrue would spend what amounts to more than a year's income to him, on something like her services. "Okay, apprentice, let's see this fabled Flair."

Bloodgrue produces a gold coin and hands it to Blue Hair. She tosses it into her coin box with the collection of copper, silver and gold coins. Un-hitching a carcass she presents it to Bloodgrue.

The apprentice dragoman accepts the chicken and then speaks candidly. "I seek your professional melee skills and warrior services, Master Blue Hair."

Blue Hair barely hesitates in giving her response. "Come see me after I sell this last chicken, apprentice."

Bloodgrue offers his arm in a deal affirmation, but Blue Hair declines to clasp. She simply watches him with a grim expression.

Feeling distraught and almost defeated for the first time in seasons, Bloodgrue walks away from Blue Hair's stall. He sits on the cobble stone pavement near the fountain so he can watch Blue Hair's stall.

Looking around, Bloodgrue notices a beggar sitting close by panhandling. "Hey, do you need food?" asks Bloodgrue.

The mature one legged jalmal grunts. "Always, my friend."

Bloodgrue nods and hands him the chicken carcass. "Here, eat well tonight. I lost my appetite."

The man takes the chicken and puts it in his sack then hobbling up on his foot he takes his possessions in readiness. Turning to Bloodgrue he says softly. "Gods-grace and good fate master, may you be blessed kindly."

Bloodgrue waves off the beggar and returns. "Maybe another day they will. You as well friend."

It is over four hours before Blue Hair receives another customer. The jalfem customer takes a quarter-of-an-hour to conclude her business.

Bloodgrue returns to stall 74 as Blue Hair is cleaning up and dismantling her pull cart stall. Bloodgrue joins in, having observed Blue Hair in the past, he knows her routine and follows through it with her. Soon they have everything clean and packed. Bloodgrue takes the poles in hand to pull the cart and says. "Where to old one?"

Blue Hair laughs, "You are going to persist aren't you. Okay, my home. You follow me; I'm not saying the address here."

They walk with Bloodgrue pulling Blue Hair's chicken stall cart, west along Elmar Road West out to Osmo Road then west along Osmo road all the way to a cottage at 1218 Osmo road.

Blue Hair informs Bloodgrue this is her farm, the whole 7.15 acres of it. She also introduces herself.

"My birth name Alandra. I grew up in the south in District 8, South Palace Hill. But I joined the King's army when I couldn't decide what to do for work at age sixteen. My family booted me out, for joining the army. I stayed with the army for sixteen years. When I was thirty-two, as a sergeant, with a child, I decided it was time to settle down with the father. I became a bounty hunter to use my army skills. I made over fifty good mark catches and collected forty-four rewards before retiring to be a merchant with my life-companion. We have held stall 74 for the last forty-eight years. I have farmed chickens the last thirty years. Fifteen years ago three assassins, trying to get to me for a mark I collected, killed my life-companion. I raised my three daughters and I keep my farm on my own. You come to me asking for my services. You don't know my services, apprentice. Not really."

Bloodgrue realises how little he knew about Blue Hair. He knew her business protocol and business in the square and some of her skills, but this was nothing of her full life. It sounds so complicated and hard to have lived. "Blue Hair, what I am asking for is lessons in use of this sailor's shortsword and the dagger. Would you do this?"

Alandra stops just inside the door of her three story field stone house. The house is forty feet on a side and field stone construction with a slate roof. The approach to the house is fifteen feet wide, paved with cobble stones. "Take the cart into the carriage house, Bloodgrue, and store it neatly. Bring the coin box inside. When you come in this door close it and take your boots off and wait for me. I will be right back. I have to inform my servant we are here and to prepare a meal for two."

It is late in the evening, half-an-hour after the day-gods have set beyond the western horizon, as the pair sit at a large dining table big enough for fourteen to sit comfortably.

"I will instruct you, but it will cost you five Dyns each session. The sessions will be on my combat practice grounds here on my estate. I will show you where tomorrow. Tonight you will sleep in the third floor guest room. Meals cost one Dyns, or two hours work for me. Work is tending my chickens and butchering, in the mornings, with me."

Bloodgrue ponders this, thinking that the work can actually be more lessons he can use. "I elect to do the work for meals. I will pay the five Dyns per session of lessons and I'll pay tonight for tomorrow's lesson."

Blue Hair accepts the five silver coins and starts to eat. "Go ahead and eat apprentice. I will show you your room after the meal. We start our session at gods-rise. If you want to eat; the meal is an hour before gods-rise."

Together, the pair socialize and eat. Bloodgrue learns more about Blue Hair and shares the little he can recall about his family, realizing he has forgotten almost everything about them.

Autumn 1 Raccoon

Today is special, not just for Bloodgrue, but the whole kingdom. It is the first full day of harvest season; the day is officially known on the records as Taumal.

For Bloodgrue it is his first official melee weapons lesson from a master. She is an actual warrior from the King's Royal army and she was an officer.

They walk along a path through the woods on Alandra's property, arriving at a site with two towers and some walls, in the far background is a building. Alandra leads Bloodgrue to the building, past a fifteen-foot-deep pit, past a thirty-foot-tall stone tower, then past a thirty-foot-tall wooden tower, past an area paved with cobble stone and an area with deep loose gravel.

Inside the small one story stone building, Blue Hair shows Bloodgrue her armor and weapons, leather and studded-leather armour, bucklers and small shields, scimitars, shortswords, daggers and spears, all neatly on racks orderly and in good repair. There are even three practice dummies stored in here.

"So all of this we may use in lessons and practice. Today I wish to assess your abilities and possibilities. I have trained professional warriors and rogues. Also, I've trained mercenaries, so we will get you some skills to use. Let's go to the cobblestone area and run through some tests and practices. Then, I will teach you some basics you need to know to be properly skilled."

After assessment the two work on Bloodgrue's skills for two hours. Bloodgrue is exhausted by the end.

Sitting on the grassy area he asks Blue Hair. "I have clients looking for employers. I have labourers and a woodworker. Have you heard of anyone seeking possible workers?"

Blue Hair, having finished up her cool down, motions for Bloodgrue to stand and follow her. It's work time. "I heard sailor Talec at 3678 Willow Road, might be hiring a labourer to look after his holding when he is on the river working. But that's the only thing I've heard in those lines. We are going to tend to my three-hundred plus chickens, and then butcher five of them. I am going to market again today. I'm late because of you. With it being festival day most of my business will be this evening anyway, so don't worry apprentice. I don't want to be with you all day anyway. We look after the chickens, then butcher. Then out on Osmo Road you are on your own again. Don't ever tell anyone where I live. Or I will rip your tongue out with my hand. Understood?"

Bloodgrue nods understanding. Together they tend to the chicken houses and the chickens, then butcher. With the five dressed chickens on her pull cart they walk out onto Osmo Road.

To be continued …

In the next episode 027, *'Cartography'*:

Bloodgrue pulls Blue Hair's cart to Elmar Road West as they talk. Bloodgrue spills the story about the Ranger and Dragon, and explains Onar's map. Blue Hair offers cartography lessons at five Dyns. Bloodgrue leaves Blue Hair at Elmar Road West and continues on his way, discovering all is not as it seemed.

Awesome! You finished episode 026 of '*Dragoman Bloodgrue*'.

Let us know what you think of it by following this link: www.inupress.ca While you are there, you can join the Inevitable Unicorn Press e-mail subscription list to receive news and updates about work from our authors such as; *Rusty Knight*, Brian Hill and Aria. When you sign up for the e-mail list, you will receive a free pdf. This free pdf changes with time. Earlier the gift was a copy of *Rusty Knight's* biography of the protagonists, the Black Swans, from his novel, *'Laret'*. Later the bonus was an episode from the serial series, *'Lanis'*.

While on the home page of InUPress.ca leave a comment, telling us what you think of our author's work or your thoughts about the website. We appreciate your time and we will respond to questions and comments.

Thank you for reading.
Yours,
Rusty Knight of Inevitable Unicorn Press.
www.inupress.ca

Dragoman Bloodgrue
Episode 027
Cartography
By Rusty Knight

Dragoman Bloodgrue
Volume V, Rulings

Welcome to our serial stories!

If you're not familiar with serials, think of them as a favorite nighttime program that continues with a new episode, only this is in print format. These are stories that don't necessarily have an end planned for them, or if they do, it's a long way off unlike many television series that we get interested in, only to have them go off air.

Serial stories are a great way to keep you entertained and on edge waiting to see what will happen next, in short enough episodes to enjoy on a lunch break, or before going to bed. Although our stories are designed to be read one episode at a time, unlike TV stories, if you just can't wait for the next episode, you can get another one any time.

Be sure to download your purchase!

It is a good idea to download the episode when you first purchase them. Then, read them at your leisure.

Please feel free to let us know what you think of our serial stories. It's a trend that may take some getting used to, but we've had positive feedback in the past with them.

Now, it's time to enjoy!
From *InUPress*

We would like to acknowledge the following for their work in the production of this series.

The author is, *Rusty Knight*
Our cover designer is, *Rusty Knight*
Our editing is by, Donna Shumaker (Aria)
Production and publication is by, *InUPress*

We at *InUPress*,
Thank you for reading *Dragoman Bloodgrue*

Dragoman Bloodgrue
Volume V, Rulings

Dragoman Bloodgrue
Volume V, Rulings

Previously in *Dragoman Bloodgrue* on **Summer 89 Raccoon**:

 Bloodgrue left the Duck and sought out Teptun Square & Market, seeking Blue Hair's guidance. She took Bloodgrue to her home, giving him lessons for a price.

Dragoman Bloodgrue

By *Rusty Knight*

Episode twenty-seven, 'Cartography'

We continue now on …

Autumn 1 Raccoon

During the festivities of Taumaul, Blue Hair and Bloodgrue are traveling along Osmo road as revellers rejoice to the gods, regaling each other with the arrival of another harvest season and the bounty of another year's growth. Flowers are shared with each other and drinks are freely consumed as revellers of the holiday mingle anywhere they are allowed. Few people actually work. Lords and estate holders open their courtyards to festival feasts and markets

Bloodgrue pulls Blue Hair's chicken cart along and tells her. "I was in the Duck of Anchor's Rest ward when a Ranger told me a fair high tale about killing a dragon and carrying the hide all the way over a desert and through the forest, across the river and then selling it to the mages. I told Master Onar and he showed me a parchment with lines and spots of colour on it. He told me it's called a map and it is used to help find locations. I wonder if you know anyone who knows about such things, old one."

Blue Hair laughs heartily, and then after calming down she picks up an ale from a street vendor and starts to answer Bloodgrue. "Yes, I know someone who knows of such things boyo. It's me. It's an art called cartography and I know it intimately. Lessons cost the same as melee lessons in price and time, when you're ready."

Bloodgrue keeps pulling the cart but smirks silently, adding the information to his bank of knowledge. He spent five years learning the alleys and streets on the north half of Mount Oryn. Onar is right. It is time to add education and knowledge if Bloodgrue wants to advance. Onar's not volunteering anything, or helping, so it's up to Bloodgrue to acquire his education.

They arrive at the Elmar Road West cross road. Bloodgrue made Blue Hair the promise to leave her be at this point. Besides, he has a goal to reach tomorrow. Tonight he needs to be at 4212 Willow Road so he can go to his goal tomorrow.

Arriving at 4212 Willow Road, well after evening meal but before the two day-gods set, Bloodgrue enters to go to his room. But before he reaches his room, he hears his name bellowed by Onar, from the office.

In the office, Bloodgrue cringes again, as Onar screams yet again, striking him on the chest with the stick. "You are to be bringing in an income, not traipsing around doing your own things. I want two Dyns apprentice. I don't care where you get it. I want two Dyns."

Bloodgrue tries to deflect the next blow, catching it with his right arm, knowing he will have a bruise but nothing worse. "I have two Dyns for you Master. Let me give it to you."

Onar stops striking Bloodgrue, but keeps the stick raised, ready to attack again. Bloodgrue, knowing he only has a count of thirty, from past experience, quickly retrieves three silver coins from his pouch and hands them to Onar. "How about three Dyns Master. Will that stop this beating?"

Onar puts the stick on the desk and takes the coins. Grudgingly he sits back in his chair. "No work, no food. Go to your room. Go out tomorrow for work and have some coins for me when you come back. Lots of coins and not just dusters, apprentice. You're buying things, you can afford my levies and fees. Go now."

Bloodgrue hurries out of the office in Onar's lull.

Entering his room, Bloodgrue mentally counts fourteen strikes from the stick, that's fourteen new bruises. He sees a small parcel on his dresser. Taking it down, he sits on his bed and shakes it. Oddly it rattles like coins, but its weight is wrong for the size to be all coins. Bloodgrue opens the parcel and immediately can smell the sweet meats. He smiles. Two pounds of sweet meats and a coin pouch and a vellum note in fourth line toydon script. Trying to decide which is more important, Bloodgrue settles on a bite of the meat then the note.

Bloodgrue, thank you for getting me this job.

It's the best job I ever had.
Teaching new recruits and older recruits; that need the lessons.
Doing administration with the House Captain and other lieutenants;
Is better than I could have dreamed of down south with my old guild.
And the apartment you found me, an hour from work is beautiful.
So, as we agreed, here is my seasonal five percent tithe, minus your guild fees and Royal and City Taxes.
It amounts to twenty-three Royal Flairs, three Dyns and one duster.

Thank you my Friend.

The next tithe will be delivered as directed on Winter 1 Raccoon.

Yours, Lieutenant Annalee of Pandora House

Bloodgrue flounders for a moment. *Did I just read correctly Flairs for one season?*

He opens the coin pouch and counts the coins.

23 Flairs
3 Dyns
1 duster

Bloodgrue places them all back in the coin pouch.
Mind gears working, the woodworker may be working soon.

Autumn 2 Raccoon

The gods breathe strongly waking Bloodgrue even earlier than he intended. Bloodgrue cooks Onar's morning meal and serves it. Bloodgrue receives only three more new bruises from strikes for making the tea too strong.

Leaving 4212 Willow Road, Bloodgrue walks firmly south to 3678 Willow Road. Knocking on the door at nearly noon, Bloodgrue hopes the sailor is home having lunch. Sure enough, the door opens and a thirty-year-old jalmal answers. "Wha the seven ells yah wan?"

Bloodgrue, taking a middle road in worker's jal, answers. "I'm lookin for sailor Talec. You know her?"

The jalmal nods. "Tha be me. Wha yah wan?"

Bloodgrue smiles his grin then answers. "I help people find work. I am Apprentice Dragoman Bloodgrue, of 4212 Willow Road. Just up a ways, about three hours walk from here. Anyway I hear you're looking for someone to tend to your place while you're out working. Is that true?"

Talec gestures for Bloodgrue to enter his house.

Bloodgrue enters a small common room and Talec serves him tea and hard tack. "I am looking for a labourer to tend to my place, yah. But they ca'na stay ere. An I ca'na feed them."

Bloodgrue drinks the bitter sailing tea, knowing its rich in something that keeps sailors healthy on long journeys. Bloodgrue doesn't mind a drink once in a while. But Talec's is particularly strong, as if it's been sitting for days. Wincing at the bitterness, Bloodgrue continues to drink smaller gulps.

"So, if I understand you, all you are offering is a wage. No food or lodging?"

Talec slams the table with an open hand. "Tha be right. One dust per da'."

Bloodgrue shakes his head, no. Setting down the empty mug, Bloodgrue responds with. "No, too low. But, I know one lad, locally, who will work for two dusters a day if you give him a day off every sixth with pay, if you aren't going to give him room and board. I believe him to be honest and reliable, though I haven't worked with him. If you have issues with him and you can't work them out together, you know my residence now. Contact me, and I will deal with it."

Talec stands and he offers his arm heartily. "Don'"

Bloodgrue smiles and stands, clasping arms, he answers. "Gods-grace and good fate, so it shall be, Sailor Talec. The lads name is Angernon. I will send him; he should be here tomorrow."

Talec smiles and even more vigorously embraces the clasp.

Bloodgrue walks along Caraway Avenue, up to the steps of Trouft House at 3617.

Entering, he looks for number sixteen and knocks, wondering if the twenty-six-year-old toymal is home.

On Bloodgrue's silent count of eighteen, Angernon opens the apartment door. Bloodgrue greets him in toy. "Gods-grace and good fate master Angernon. I have some news for you, may I enter?"

Angernon excitedly moves to the side and says eagerly. "Yes! Yes, of coarse dragoman, come in. I heard about Jered. Is my news the same?"

Bloodgrue enters the small common room with its table and two chairs. There is a brazier on the counter with some cookware. Some food stuffs sit on the counter.

Angernon busily starts making tea after closing the door.

Soon the two start drinking the hot tea as they sit at the table. "I have a verbal contract with Sailor Talec at 3678 Willow Road. You start tomorrow. You will be tending to his property when he is working. You will receive only two dusters a day ... No room or board or bonuses. But you get every sixth day off with pay. You will send me nine dusters on the first of Winter Raccoon and the first of every season, as long as you are employed by Master Talec at this wage. I reside at 4212 Willow Road, if you have forgotten."

Angernon smiles and offers Bloodgrue. "Stay, have evening meal with me, Dragoman."

Bloodgrue nods and offers to clasp arms. Without hesitation Angernon clasps. Bloodgrue asks. "May I stay the night on the floor?"

Angernon points to a cot. "Please use my brother's cot. He is away a few days."

Autumn 3 Raccoon

Arriving at stall 74 nearly halfway between mid-day and evening meal, Bloodgrue is ecstatic to find Blue Hair still here. He rushes over to her as she is walking around idly without customers. Bloodgrue addresses Blue Hair. "Five Dyns for a chicken, please."

Blue Hair unhooks one of the two remaining carcasses as Bloodgrue counts out five Dyns.

They exchange items and Bloodgrue says to Blue Hair. "I want cartography lessons. At least teach me what cartography is and some basics."

Blue Hair places the coins in her box and then looks at Bloodgrue. "Tonight, after I deal with the last carcass. And no you can't buy it."

Bloodgrue snaps his fingers in exaggeration, as he laughs. "Damn! Seven Hells! Okay, I'll wait."

He goes to the fountain and seeing the one-legged panhandler again, Bloodgrue approaches. "If I am going to be giving you my chickens, at least tell me your name."

The panhandler rises to his one foot and replies. "It used to be Rufus Goodall. Just call me Rufus. A Mountain Lizard got my leg, my friend. Thank you. I saw you buy these from Blue Hair. So I know they aren't cheap. I owe you something. If you want a set of eyes here, mine are open for you. Who are you?"

Bloodgrue hands Rufus the chicken. "I have titles. But you can know me as Bloodgrue. Apprentice Dragoman Bloodgrue, or Pandora Blood of First Rank. These are my titles, but Rufus, just call me Bloodgrue. Have a good evening. Gods-grace and good fate my friend, I will take you up on your offer."

They clasp arms and Rufus places the chicken in his pack, then with the aid of an old crutch he starts to hobble off.

Bloodgrue calls after him. "Rufus. Wait."

Bloodgrue takes a Flair from his pouch and keeping it concealed in his hand, he palms it to Rufus just as Luenen taught him.

Rufus has tears in his eyes as he silently hobbles away headed east.

As Bloodgrue turns around to watch Blue Hair, a young jalmal grabs Bloodgrue's arm.

Bloodgrue assess the youth. He looks to be about twenty, shorter than average but with average build.

"Boy, you shouldn't be carrying a sailor's sword from Dendar, unless you are a sailor from Dendar. Are you from Dendar? You don't walk like a sailor." says the youth.

Bloodgrue jerks free. Even being only seventeen, Bloodgrue doesn't like to be manhandled by anyone and being grabbed on the bruises made by Onar, made the issue worse. Thus it is making Bloodgrue belligerent already. "Seven Hells, no I'm not from Dendar. And I ain't no sailor. And there's no way you get my sword. I earned it through hard work."

The young man curses in jal, then moves aggressively, reaching for the sword. "You aren't a sailor; you can't have that sword. My father is a Captain of a Barge. He is Captain Ferrec of the North Wind. I'm taking it for him."

Bloodgrue backs away before the young jalmal can grasp the sword.

The sailor's son curses again and draws his dagger menacingly.

Blue Hair said to only draw the sword in self defense. Bloodgrue sees this as such a situation. He draws the sword hesitantly, but not clumsily. Bloodgrue feels comfortable with the sword after Blue Hair's work with him.

The young man rushes Bloodgrue, striking out with some skill with the dagger.

Dragoman Bloodgrue
Volume V, Rulings

Bloodgrue lets Blue Hair's lessons flow naturally, without trying too hard to focus. The shortsword drives out at the rushing lad piercing his chest, before the dagger can find Bloodgrue.

The attacker falls and Blue Hair runs over cursing in more languages than Bloodgrue's ever heard.

She starts dealing with the bleeding wound immediately, professionally tending to it with skill Bloodgrue never knew she had. After several minutes, Blue Hair has the bleeding stopped. But the youth has lost consciousness, though he still breaths.

Bloodgrue looks among the onlookers and pulling aside a toymal he says. "Here are two dusters. Get the City Watch quickly."

Bloodgrue turns back to the unconscious youth and Blue Hair.

Blue Hair stands up and looks at Bloodgrue. "That is the lethality of what I taught you. You used it, now own it. You look after this. My healer's fee is one Flair. It is due now. The Watch will have questions and may lay charges. I don't know what all happened. I couldn't hear it all. So be prepared."

Bloodgrue fishes a Flair out of his pouch of dwindling coins and gives it to Blue Hair. He then cleans the sword on the youth's tunic trying not to disturb the wound's dressing. Pocketing the boy's coin pouch as unobserved as possible, in the manner taught to him by Luenen. It felt heavy but it could all be dusters. He will have to check later, not here.

Six City Watch arrive quickly. A toyfem addresses Bloodgrue. "I'm Private Elisa, are you responsible here?"

Bloodgrue stands tall and firm as he answers. "Yes. I was the one who dropped this man while I was defending myself from his attack."

Elisa nods. She looks over the body and sees the dagger still nearby. Looking over the wound dressing and confirming the youth is still breathing, she returns to Bloodgrue. "Do you have any witnesses as to what happened and who are you?"

Bloodgrue bows nobly to the private, as if bowing to a knight. "I am Apprentice Dragoman Bloodgrue. I see no one here, who was here when I was attacked. Blue Hair is the healer who saved the man's life, but she noticed after I defended myself."

Elisa nods. "Okay Bloodgrue, I've seen you around and haven't had issues with you before. You helped with the capture of a known criminal on the docks. You stayed here to own your handiwork and you kept him alive. So I am going to take your words for this. But, we will have to deal with him now. It would have been easier if he were dead. But less moral. So I give you credit for doing the right thing. Thus, I am only going to charge you a levy of one Flair, due now. Or you will be taken into custody to go to the goal for twenty days."

Bloodgrue sighs, this he can deal with. He presents a Flair from his pouch, leaving him two. "Thank you Private Elisa. I try to avoid such issues and will try more diplomacy in the future to avoid clean up. I will try to make clean up easier in the future if it happens again though, if you prefer."

Elisa smiles as she puts the gold coin in her pouch. "I personally don't prefer, Bloodgrue. This is better."

Blue Hair finally deals with her last chicken after evening meal time. Together the two, Bloodgrue and Blue Hair, travel to 1218 Osmo Road with Bloodgrue pulling the chicken cart.

He places it properly this time in the carriage house. Taking the coin box into the house, he hands it to the now clean Blue Hair. Bloodgrue takes his shoes off and puts them on the rack. As Bloodgrue starts to head to the south door to the common room, Blue Hair takes Bloodgrue's arm.

"Follow me student. We go to my office now. I had to wake my servant. So she will be a while getting our meal ready. It is after mid-night." Blue Hairs says softly to Bloodgrue.

She leads Bloodgrue to the west door and into a twenty foot by twenty-foot room with a fully carpeted floor. Tapestries and paintings adorn the walls. There are three windows to the outside. In the one wall is a small fireplace. Several bookshelves are mounted on the walls with nearly four hundred texts and thirty rolled up maps. There is a six-foot-tall marble statue of Stonewire and a four-foot-high alabaster statue of a horse. Lanterns are mounted on the walls. But what dominates the room is the large oak desk and padded oak desk chair with arms. There are also six oak padded guest chairs near the desk.

Bloodgrue stands a few moments in awe at the opulence here. Again, Blue Hair has surprised him. Looking at the walls, Bloodgrue sees what must be a map. But, it is much more complicated and detailed than the one Onar showed him. It is mounted on the wall and is four feet square.

Bloodgrue finally closes his mouth long enough to look at Blue Hair. "Who are you?" is all he can say.

To be continued …

In the next episode 028, *'Merchant Terace'*:

Local merchant Terace hires Bloodgrue to escort her daughter into Velan district for her journeyman weaver testing. On the journey, Bloodgrue encounters an over-enthusiastic merchant thug, who Bloodgrue and Noah previously fleeced of a pack of Flairs, with which Noah bought Red Square. The thug wants to deal with Bloodgrue about the issue, but less than peacefully.

Dragoman Bloodgrue
Volume V, Rulings

Awesome! You finished episode 027 of '*Dragoman Bloodgrue*'.

Let us know what you think of it by following this link: www.inupress.ca While you are there, you can join the Inevitable Unicorn Press e-mail subscription list to receive news and updates about work from our authors such as; *Rusty Knight*, Brian Hill and Aria. When you sign up for the e-mail list, you will receive a free pdf. This free pdf changes with time. Earlier the gift was a copy of *Rusty Knight's* biography of the protagonists, the Black Swans, from his novel, *'Laret'*. Later in 2016, the bonus was an episode from the serial series, *'Lanis'*.

While at InUPress.ca leave a comment, telling us what you think of our author's work or your thoughts about the website. We appreciate your time and we will respond to questions and comments.

Thank you for reading.
Yours,
Rusty Knight of Inevitable Unicorn Press.
www.inupress.ca

Dragoman
Bloodgrue
Episode 028
Merchant Terace

By Rusty Knight

Dragoman Bloodgrue
Volume V, Rulings

Welcome to our serial stories!

If you're not familiar with serials, think of them as a favorite nighttime program that continues with a new episode, only this is in print format. These are stories that don't necessarily have an end planned for them, or if they do, it's a long way off unlike many television series that we get interested in, only to have them go off air.

Serial stories are a great way to keep you entertained and on edge waiting to see what will happen next, in short enough episodes to enjoy on a lunch break, or before going to bed. Although our stories are designed to be read one episode at a time, unlike TV stories, if you just can't wait for the next episode, you can get another one any time.

Be sure to download your purchase!

It is a good idea to download the episode when you first purchase them. Then, read them at your leisure.

Please feel free to let us know what you think of our serial stories. It's a trend that may take some getting used to, but we've had positive feedback in the past with them.

Now, it's time to enjoy!
From *InUPress*,

We would like to acknowledge the following for their work in the production of this series.

Our author us, *Rusty Knight*
Our cover designer is, *Rusty Knight*
Our editing is by, Donna Shumaker (Aria)
Production and publication is by, *InUPress*

We at *InUPress*,
Thank you for reading *Dragoman Bloodgrue*

Dragoman Bloodgrue
Volume V, Rulings

Previously in **Dragoman Bloodgrue** on **Autumn 1 Raccoon**:

Bloodgrue left Blue Hair to seek employment for one of his clients. While out, Bloodgrue gets into a sword fight with a barge Captain's son who tried to take Bloodgrue's Dendar Sailor's sword.

Dragoman Bloodgrue
Volume V, Rulings

Dragoman Bloodgrue

By *Rusty Knight*

Episode twenty-eight, 'Merchant Terace'

We continue now on …

Autumn 4 Raccoon

Bloodgrue wakes in the guest bed at Blue Hair's estate. He is somewhat rested after a short sleep. He had an exhausting night.

Getting to 1218 Osmo Road after mid-night, the two spent over two hours in Blue Hair's study, where Bloodgrue learned the basics about cartography and discovered how much there is to learn about Blue Hair and her knowledge. After exhaustive studies that barely even touched on the art of cartography, they went to the dining room and ate evening meal.

Blue Hair then shuffled Bloodgrue off to the third floor bedroom, informing him he had six hours in which he could sleep before morning meal.

Bloodgrue finishes on the chamber pot and hurries down the circular stair case to the ground floor and then over into the dining room. He finds Blue Hair eating an apple with pancakes and hot syrup. There is a jug of milk on the table and a setting for Bloodgrue.

Blue Hair smiles evilly. "You almost missed. You have half an hour to finish up and be ready to tend the chickens."

…..

It took the two of them over two hours to tend to the chickens and butcher five. Bloodgrue pulled Blue Hair's chicken cart for six hours to get it to stall 74 in Teptun Square & Market. He looks around to find several folks waiting for Blue Hair and decides to wait and see if any business transfers his way today.

"Bloodgrue come here." calls Blue Hair after she talks with her first customer.

Bloodgrue approaches calmly but rapidly.

"Yes, Master Blue Hair. How may I be of assistance?" Bloodgrue enquires as he approaches the three people standing at the stall.

Blue Hair points to the mature jalfem and says professionally to Bloodgrue. "This is Merchant Terace. Her daughter needs to go to the Weavers Guild Hall in Velan district to test for her journeyman certification. I am recommending you as her escort. Can you get her safely to the destination?"

Bloodgrue straightens up firmly in his posture and answers with a grin. "I can. I know the address and roads. We can walk to 4212 Willow Road to stay the night then continue to the Nobleman's Rest tomorrow and the Weaver's the day after for testing. Then I can escort her back."

Terace looks at Bloodgrue in disgust and utters. "You are a simple commoner; why would I trust you with my daughter's safety? How do I trust you?"

Bloodgrue thinks a moment then answers. "You can't until I work for you, or you ask someone you already trust who knows me. So give me this chance to work for you after you talk with Blue Hair. I will tell you I have been a dragoman five years and never harmed a client or lost a client. I have never become so lost it cost my client. I will wait with your daughter while you talk privately with Blue Hair, if you like?"

Terace smiles and nods, while motioning aside Blue Hair.

While the two elders talk, Bloodgrue motions the daughter closer. "I am Apprentice Dragoman Bloodgrue. You are the one who will have to trust me. It will be for at least six days if you go with me. The cost is one Dyns a day plus food and lodging for the trip. I will do my best to keep you safe on this trip. It's usually very uneventful. I've gone a few times to the area. The last time I went with Sir Genner, a Knight. We will have to equip you properly for travel though. Will you travel with me?"

The woman has all the markings of a halfer. She is shorter, has violet eyes, lighter hair and pale skin. She looks to be nearly forty years old, thus to Bloodgrue in his mind he questions her state of mind, if she is going for her journeyman certification this late in life.

She answers Bloodgrue in a slight drawl, slower than most would. "My name is Ela and yes I do trust you Bloodgrue to get me to the weaver's hall and return here. But momma is over-protective cause papa was a toymal and she thinks I can't look after myself. We'll tell her you're taking me."

Her speech confirms for Bloodgrue that Ela is slow of mind to some degree. But not everyone burns a full flame candle. Some only burn half a flame or small candle. Ela might be burning three quarter size candle. But that is alright. "Let's wait and see what they decide, Ela."

It takes twenty minutes, then Blue Hair and Terace return. Terace extends her arm to Bloodgrue. "What are your rates Dragoman? I hear your proficient with your sword, so you can escort Ela."

Bloodgrue clasps arms and firmly replies. "One Dyns per day, plus food and lodging, Master Terace. I haven't had trouble yet on this run. Ela will need about five Dyns worth of gear to make the trip before we set out as well."

Merchant Terace looks at Blue Hair while raising her right eyebrow and frowning.

Blue Hair nods to Terace.

Terace removes her coin pouch and gives Bloodgrue five Dyns of her coins.

"I will be right back with the gear." says Bloodgrue.

Ten minutes later, Bloodgrue returns with an eight-litre waterskin filled with water and a pack with hard tack and a knife. He hands these to Ela and hands Terace seven dusters. "Okay, ready to go. First place we go is 4212 Willow Road for an overnight stay."

The duo makes good time and arrive at 4212 Willow Road only a few minutes after gods-set. Bloodgrue introduces Ela to Master Onar, then cooks them a meal and settles Ela into the guest room.

Autumn 5 Raccoon

The duo leaves 4212 Willow Road after gods-rise, fighting the heavy breath of the gods, with partial cover in the sphere. They walk long through the day, arriving at the Nobleman's Rest only an hour before the day-gods set.

Stepping into the Nobleman's, Bloodgrue soon has two rooms for them, with meals.

Autumn 6 Raccoon

It has been raining for hours as Bloodgrue enters the tavern of the Nobleman's Rest. The day-gods haven't breeched the horizon, if you could see the horizon of the sphere. Which it can't be seen because of the sphere cover.

In the tavern is a nervous Ela waiting to go for her testing. The innkeeper is ready to serve customers and there is another familiar face Bloodgrue hasn't seen in a few seasons.

In fact, Bloodgrue had hoped never to see again.

"Good day Dragoman Bloodgrue. When I heard you were here, I simply had to come see for myself. And you came bearing gifts I see, and with unarmed defenceless company. Why is she so nervous, shaking like a little puppy like that?" he says.

Bloodgrue walks close to the short man. Terri, the shortest adult jalmal Bloodgrue recalls, is the roundest for his height as well. He must be over two hundred pounds, but only five feet four inches. Terri doesn't look to have a lot of muscle either. "Well, merchant Terri. Are you alone, or are you going to gang up on a lone dragoman?"

Terri smiles for Bloodgrue. "Dragoman, I work alone. When I tried to buy Western Madison I was working alone and I am here alone. That was my pack of coins you and your friend took. I want it all back, plus interest."

Bloodgrue frowns for Terri and replies. "I don't have fifty Flairs, Terri."

Terri swings a fist at Bloodgrue, but Blood backs up avoiding the blow. "That was fifty-five you imp. And I will take what coin you have now as interest and you get me my fifty-five, plus ten more as compensation. Now hand over your pouch, or I'll take it."

Bloodgrue recalls the Teptun Square altercation with the barge captain's son. It was too easy. With a piecing to the abdomen, the sword fell the boy quickly. There, Blue Hair saved the boys life. There is no one here to save this man's life. Bloodgrue refrains from drawing the sword yet. He backs away. "I'm not giving you anything, Terri."

Terri lunges at Bloodgrue. "Yes you are, or I'm just going to take it."

Bloodgrue steps out of the way.

Terri expertly pulls out his knife and begins stalking Bloodgrue with a vengeance. "You don't get a choice Bloodgrue. Alive or dead, your coin pouch, sword, and belongings are mine."

Bloodgrue, seeing no alternative, draws his Sailor's shortsword.

The innkeeper exits the tavern going out onto the streets running.

Terri lunges at Bloodgrue with his knife.

Bloodgrue thrusts out at him with the sword.

Neither man draws any blood.

Terri's arm quickly comes over Bloodgrue's sword arm slashing open Bloodgrue's face.

They retreat from each other for a moment. With blood trickling down Bloodgrue's face, he sees there really isn't an option. He closes with Terri. Seeing an opening, he thrust into Terri's ribs breaking them. Terri falls to the floor in agony, dropping his knife. Bloodgrue kicks the knife away and watches as life bleeds away from Terri. Three minutes of unconscious bleeding and Terri ceases to breathe.

Bloodgrue has emptied all but three dusters from Terri's coin pouch into his own. Otherwise, the body is undisturbed.

About five minutes later the innkeeper returns with City Watch.

Three city Watch enter the tavern. There are two sergeants and a private. Their leader, a jalfem approaches Bloodgrue, while the other sergeant checks the body.

"Gods-grace and good fate, I am Sergeant Lena. So, you were just engaged by this man. Tell me in your words what happened." She says.

Bloodgrue tenderly wipes at his wound with a table cloth. "Gods-grace and good fate Sergeant Lena. I am Apprentice Dragoman Bloodgrue; I am escorting Apprentice Weaver Ela to her journeyman certification testing. I came to the tavern from my room, to start my day, when merchant Terri here started in, saying I owed him fifty-five Flairs and he wants everything I have with me now. He assaulted me, then drew his knife to attack and said he was going to kill me to take everything. This is the result."

Lena nods. Looking at Bloodgrue's sword she hands it back. "I haven't seen one of those specific ones in years. You look after it well. It will kill a man faster than most. Yes, I see you know how to use it too. That's military use. What unit are you from?"

Bloodgrue cleans the blade off with the same table cloth and answers before sheathing his sword. "I must confess; I take training from a weapons master that trains Royal Military. I have no unit. Her name is Blue Hair."

The sergeant stops and looks at Bloodgrue questioningly. "Blue Hair is training you?"

Somewhat confused at the way Lena asked the question, as if she is asking in deep respect, Bloodgrue shrugs and answers. "Yes, she is my teacher."

All three City Watch approach Bloodgrue and salute, then extend their arms.

Even more confused, Bloodgrue simply clasps arms.

Lena goes back to business. "Master Bloodgrue, there is nothing more we can do here. The man is dead and stood no chance of recovery. You must tend to his removal and Right of Passage. For your part in this, you are responsible for a fee of one Flair or thirty days in the Velan goal. This must be paid now. I am sorry Master; you are a Velan outter, even though your mentor is Master Blue Hair."

Dragoman Bloodgrue
Volume V, Rulings

Bloodgrue nods with a smile as he can easily tend to this. He gives Lena a Flair. As he does so she sighs heavily and smiles, again offering her arm. Bloodgrue clasps her arm.

The City Watch gone, Bloodgrue ponders what to do with the body. Then he pulls out his pouch and offers the innkeeper a Dyns. "If you can quickly have priests of Stonewire here to tend to the body, this is yours."

The innkeeper smiles, takes the offered coin and exits the tavern and inn.

Half-an-hour later, the Innkeeper returns with six priests of Stonewire.

Bloodgrue greets them. "Gods-grace and good fate masters. I seem to have had an issue. This man seems to have passed away. Can you see to it he finds Stonewire?"

The Father nods and looks the body over. Standing, he addresses Bloodgrue. "Stonewire's Blessing my son. Is this your work?"

Bloodgrue sighs and nods. "Yes, Father."

The priest nods. "You did a fairly permanent job of it son. We will give him Right of Passage before he can walk again. It will cost fifteen Dyns. Pay now."

Bloodgrue sighs in relief. He has heard of priests charging as much as ten Flairs for one ceremony. He counts out one Flair and five Dyns. "Do you need me anymore Father?"

The priest waves away Bloodgrue and they collect the body and leave.

Bloodgrue hands the innkeeper three Dyns. "We need rooms and meals for tonight. I'm not supplying anymore entertainment though."

Bloodgrue washes his wound and rinses it with hard alcohol to avoid bloodfires.

Bloodgrue escorts Ela to the Weavers Hall and she does her testing. In the evening they trek back to the Nobleman's Rest.

To be continued …

In the next episode 029, '*Fire on Willow Road*':

Bloodgrue and Ela are returning to Teptun Square & Market when they are interrupted by fires. Bloodgrue attempts to make rescues, but lives are lost.

InUPress

Dragoman Bloodgrue
Volume V, Rulings

As producer at *InUPress.ca* and author of the *Dragoman Bloodgrue* serial short-story series, I thank you for reading *Dragoman Bloodgrue Volume 5: Rulings* by *Rusty Knight*.

The *Dragoman Bloodgrue Volume* series will be continued in February 2017 with *Bloodgrue Volume 6: Servile*

These can be found at *InUPress.ca*, *Amazon* and *Kobo:*

Bloodgrue Volume 1: Fare Where?
Bloodgrue Volume 2: Breaths
Bloodgrue Volume 3: Business
Bloodgrue Volume 4: Attractions
Bloodgrue Volume 5: Rulings

As publisher at *InUPress.ca* and author of the *Dragoman Bloodgrue*, *Markus* and *Lanis* serial short-story series I thank you for reading our series.

Yours,
Rusty Knight and *InUPress.ca*

90